DINOFOURS®

LET'S GO SLEDDING!

To Alexander "Papa" Stern
—S.M.

Text copyright © 2002 by Scholastic Inc.
Illustrations copyright © 2002 by Hans Wilhelm, Inc.
All rights reserved. Published by Scholastic Inc.
SCHOLASTIC, CARTWHEEL BOOKS, DINOFOURS, and associated logos
are trademarks and/or registered trademarks of Scholastic Inc.

Library of Congress Cataloging-in-Publication Data

Metzger, Steve.
    Let's Go Sledding! / by Steve Metzger ; illustrated by Hans Wilhelm.
        p. cm. — (Dinofours)
    "Cartwheel Books."
    Summary: On a perfect day for sledding, the Dinofours find out that it can be fun to do something together.
    ISBN 0-439-29571-8 (pbk.)
        [1. Sledding—Fiction. 2. Cooperativeness—Fiction. 3. Dinosaurs—Fiction.] I. Wilhelm, Hans, 1945- ill.
II. Title.

PZ7.M56775 Le 2002
[E]—dc21   2001032083

10 9 8 7 6 5 4 3 2 1   02   03   04   05   06

Printed in the U.S.A.   24
First printing, January 2002

LET'S GO SLEDDING!

by Steve Metzger
Illustrated by Hans Wilhelm

Cartwheel
·B·O·O·K·S· ®

SCHOLASTIC INC.
New York   Toronto   London   Auckland   Sydney
Mexico City   New Delhi   Hong Kong   Buenos Aires

It had snowed all night long.

The next morning, Tara and her father walked to school.

"Look at that tree!" said Tara. "The branches are all white!"

"Yes," said Tara's father. "And take a look at that car. You can't even tell what color it is."

Tara and her father walked on, noticing the many things that were covered with snow.

Just before they arrived at school, Tara said, "I hope we take a trip to Dino Hill today. I really want to go sledding!"

When Tara opened the door, she saw all the other children
laughing and talking excitedly to one another.
"What's going on?" asked Tara.
"We're going to Dino Hill!" said Albert.
"Wow!" said Tara.

"Yes," said Mrs. Dee. "Everyone wants to go sledding on Dino Hill. I hope you do, too."

"I do! I do!" Tara said in a loud voice. "When are we going?"

"Right now," Mrs. Dee replied. "Are you ready?"

"I sure am!" said Tara. "Bye-bye, Daddy."

"Good-bye, Tara," said her father as he walked out the door. "Have a great time!"

"Please line up by the door," said Mrs. Dee to the children.

"I'm the Line Leader today," said Danielle, looking at the Job Chart.

"And I'll be the caboose," said Joshua.

"There are some sleds in a storage shed at the top of Dino Hill," said Mrs. Dee, "but they haven't been used in quite a while. I hope they're still in good shape."

JOB CHART
Clean Tables
ALBERT
Line Leader
DANIELLE
Water the
JOSHUA
Snack

When everyone was ready, Mrs. Dee
took the class outside to the trail that led
to Dino Hill.

As they walked along, Tara sang this
song:

Snow, snow, so much snow—
Everything is white!
Snow, snow, I love snow—
It's such a pretty sight!

When they reached the bottom of Dino Hill, the children looked up.

"It's so tall!" said Danielle.

"Yeah! Dino Hill looks like a mountain!" Albert added.

"Hey, it's not so big," said Brendan. "Watch me. I can run all the way to the top."

Brendan began to run up Dino Hill.

"Don't get too far ahead of us, Brendan," said Mrs. Dee.

But after running for only a little while, Brendan stopped. Huffing and puffing, he said, "Mrs. Dee is right. I shouldn't get too far ahead."

Finally, everyone made it to the top.

Looking down, Tara said, "Everything looks so beautiful."

"Here's the storage shed," said Mrs. Dee. "I'll take out the sleds. It's important that you stay here until I get back."

"Okay, Mrs. Dee," the children said together.

As soon as Mrs. Dee went inside the shed, Brendan began making snowballs and throwing them at the other children.

"Hey!" said Joshua. "Don't throw snowballs at me!"

"Cut it out, Brendan!" said Tracy.

"What's the matter?" asked Brendan. "Don't you like snowball fights? *I* do."

All at once, the other children began throwing snowballs at Brendan.

"Stop it! Stop it!" Brendan exclaimed. "I was only kidding."

Just then, Mrs. Dee came out of the storage shed. "I'm sorry," she said, "but only *one* of the sleds is in good enough shape to ride on. You'll have to take turns."

"I'm first," Danielle called out, "because I'm the Line Leader!"

"No, *I'm* first," said Tracy, "because I have a big sister!"

"No, *I'm* first," said Albert, "because my name begins with an A, and A is the first letter of the alphabet!"

The children began calling out reasons why they should go on the sled first...except Tara.

"Stop!" said Tara. "It's too nice and snowy to fight. Why don't we all go down Dino Hill together? Look! It's a really big sled."

"Tara's right," said Joshua.

"That's a great idea, Tara!" said Mrs. Dee.

"Well, what are we waiting for?" asked Danielle.

In an instant, all of the children jumped onto the sled. "We're ready,
Mrs. Dee!"

Mrs. Dee gave the sled a push, and down the hill they went...faster
and faster.

"*Wheeeeeee!*" shouted the children as they held on to one another.

At the bottom of Dino Hill, the sled slowed down, then stopped.
Mrs. Dee ran to greet them.

"How was it?" asked Mrs. Dee.
"Terrific!" said Danielle.
"Fun!" said Albert.
"And it was all Tara's idea," said Mrs. Dee.

All the children cheered for Tara.

"Thank you, Tara," said Tracy. "Now, let's do it again."

So the children went down Dino Hill again...and again...and again!

After many rides, it was time to return to school.
On their way back, Tara sang a new song:

It's fun to sled down Dino Hill—
Faster, faster, wheeeeeee!
It's better when I'm with my friends—
Better than just me!